WELCOME TO
PASSPORT TO READING
A beginning reader's ticket to a brand-new world!

Every book in this program is designed to build read-along and read-alone skills, level by level, through engaging and enriching stories. As the reader turns each page, he or she will become more confident with new vocabulary, sight words, and comprehension.

These PASSPORT TO READING levels will help you choose the perfect book for every reader.

READING TOGETHER
Read short words in simple sentence structures together to begin a reader's journey.

READING OUT LOUD
Encourage developing readers to sound out words in more complex stories with simple vocabulary.

READING INDEPENDENTLY
Newly independent readers gain confidence reading more complex sentences with higher word counts.

READY TO READ MORE
Readers prepare for chapter books with fewer illustrations and longer paragraphs.

This book features sight words from the educator-supported Dolch Sight Words List. This encourages the reader to recognize commonly used vocabulary words, increasing reading speed and fluency.

For more information, please visit passporttoreadingbooks.com.

Enjoy the journey!

Little, Brown and Company

Hachette Book Group
1290 Avenue of the Americas, New York, NY 10104
Visit us at lb-kids.com

Little, Brown and Company is a division of Hachette Book Group, Inc.
The Little, Brown name and logo are trademarks of Hachette Book Group, Inc.

The publisher is not responsible for websites (or their content) that are not owned by the publisher.

First Edition: November 2016

Library of Congress Control Number: 2016938007

ISBN 978-0-316-27432-6

10 9 8 7 6 5 4 3 2

CW

PRINTED IN THE UNITED STATES OF AMERICA

Passport to Reading titles are leveled by independent reviewers applying the standards developed by Irene Fountas
and Gay Su Pinnell in *Matching Books to Readers: Using Leveled Books in Guided Reading*, Heinemann, 1999.

Licensed By:

TRANSFORMERS
ROBOTS IN DISGUISE

A New Adventure

By Steve Foxe

L B

LITTLE, BROWN AND COMPANY
New York   Boston

The Autobots come from Cybertron.

So do the evil Decepticons.

When their prison ship crashes on Earth, hundreds of Decepticons escape.

Optimus Prime sends Bumblebee,
Strongarm, and Sideswipe to Earth.
They will protect the planet!

Bumblebee is the leader of
the Autobots on Earth.
He can change into a yellow sports car.

Bee always does his best.

He wants Optimus Prime to be proud.

Bumblebee works to make
these bots into a great team!

Sideswipe has speed and style.
He doesn't always follow
Bumblebee's orders.
He is a rebel.

But Sideswipe is always there
for his friends.
He can outrace almost anyone
in his race car mode.

Strongarm is a cop.

She always follows the law.

She is very serious about her job.

But she will bend the rules
to keep people safe.
Her police SUV vehicle mode
matches her love for justice!

Grimlock does not like thinking.
He prefers STOMPING bad guys!

In his Tyrannosaurus rex form, no one can stop him!

Fixit is a Mini-Con.

He helps track down the Decepticons.

When the Autobots get hurt,

he fixes them.

He is a good teammate.

Bumblebee and the others
live in a scrapyard.
They track down the
bad guys in Crown City.

Bumblebee and his friends
are robots in disguise.
They fight to protect
the human race!

Denny Clay is a human.
So is his son, Rusty.
Denny owns the scrapyard
where the bots live.

They know about the Autobots
and Decepticons.
They help Team Bee when
they can.

Optimus Prime is the Autobot leader on Cybertron.

Optimus trusts his former partner
Bumblebee to lead the Autobots
on Earth.
Optimus becomes a semitruck.
He helps the bots
track down the
unleashed Decepticons!

Drift is a bounty hunter. Usually he works alone. But he joined the Autobots' worthy cause.

Drift fights with sharp swords!
His Mini-Con students are named
Jetstorm and Slipstream.

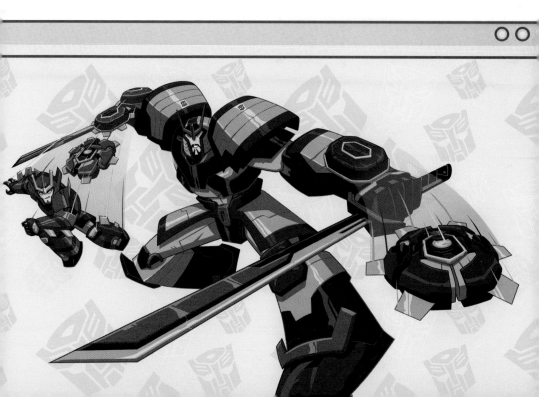

Slipstream and Jetstorm started out as crooks.

But Drift taught them the value of honor and respect.

These two small samurai like
to play games and have fun.
They have helped the Autobots
get out of some tight spots!

Windblade was sent to Earth thousands of years ago.

She is the only bot who can fly. Windblade wants to stop the Decepticons once and for all!

Over three hundred Decepticons escaped when the prison ship crashed.
But only Steeljaw and his band of bullies have threatened the Autobots.

They want to take over the Earth!

The Autobot heroes have captured many of the Decepticons. But there are still plenty more who remain on the loose.

Good thing Bumblebee and the rest of his team are here to rev up, roll out, and protect the planet!

When an Autobot prison ship
crashes on Earth, hundreds of
Decepticons escape. Now it's up
to Bumblebee and his team to
find the bad guys. Learn about
your favorite heroes and foes in
this exciting book!

CHECKPOINTS IN THIS BOOK ✔

WORD COUNT	GUIDED READING LEVEL	NUMBER OF DOLCH SIGHT WORDS
449	K	75

PASSPORT TO READING 1 READING TOGETHER

PASSPORT TO READING 2 READING OUT LOUD

PASSPORT TO READING 3 READING INDEPENDENTLY

PASSPORT TO READING 4 READY TO READ MORE

Licensed By:

HASBRO and its logo
TRANSFORMERS,
TRANSFORMERS
ROBOTS IN DISGUISE,
the logo and all related
characters are trademarks of Hasbro
and are used with permission. © 2016
Hasbro. All Rights Reserved.
Cover design by Ching Chan
PRINTED IN THE U.S.A.
TRANSFORMERS.com

Look inside for more about
Passport to Reading!
Visit passporttoreadingbooks.com

L B

VISIT US AT
lb-kids.com

$4.99 US / $6.49 CAN

ISBN 978-0-316-27432-6

50499

EAN

9 780316 274326